CW01082816

IciKILL

IciKILL

RICK E. CUTTS

Library of Congress Control Number:		2024920953
ISBN:	Hardcover	979-8-3694-3091-0
	Softcover	979-8-3694-3092-7
	eBook	979-8-3694-3093-4

Print information available on the last page.

Rev. date: 09/30/2024

To order additional copies of this book, contact:
Xlibris
844-714-8691
www.Xlibris.com
Orders@Xlibris.com
863057

Acknowledgments

Writing books is an amazing amount of work. It's positively a task. Writing is very rewarding once you see the finished product. I would like to thank my wife and family for being so supportive and encouraging. Thank you to all those that have supported my writing and stories and ask me "when will the next book come out". I truly appreciate everyone a lot and I can't wait for everyone to enjoy iciKILL. I must also thank God. I know that it seems like people say it all the time just to say it. I truly believe that without God there is no way I could do any of this at all.

Thank you!

Introduction

Leo is heading out of his office to his car. Out of nowhere a killer jumps out and with an icicle attacks Leo. After impaling Leo with the icicle, the killer escapes after eliminating the footprints with a hand dryer. Now with no murder weapon after the icicle melts and no physical evidence of any footprints how will the Detective and CSI agent be able to solve this crime? Can they solve it. It looks like a death of natural causes.

Follow Detective Jackson and CSI agent Adders as they go on an amazing journey that takes readers through multiple twist and turns. Will they be able to find out whether people are just dropping dead of natural causes or is something more sinister going on. Who's behind it? Why is it happening?

IciKILL will truly have everyone guessing all the way to the very end.

Just a cold winter evening. There is a huge office building. The building seems to be completely empty. You can hear a little bit of wind outside whistling through the windows. There is one light on in the entire building on an upper-level floor. Outside the only office where the light is on is a gold plaque on the door that says "Director Leo". Inside the office is very neat and structured. You can see a stack of papers on one desk with a label that says, "complete". There is another stack of papers with a Label that says "working". There is also a bin with a few pieces of paper with a label that says "Maybe". The office has a very vintage look to it. All the furniture is a heavy, dark red wood with a large desk. There is a computer with three screens and the smell of the room is a mixture of wood and fresh linen. There is a guy at his desk working away. His name is Leo. Leo is one of the top executives in the company. Leo is the type that will not leave the office until a task is complete. Often, he is the last one out of the office or sometimes falls asleep in his office. That is not a problem because inside his office is a nice large couch that he sometimes lays on to sleep. Leo is a very task-driven person. There has never been a deadline that Leo didn't make. Leo has his glasses on top of his head. He leans back in his chair, rubs his eyes, leans back forward. He grabs the glass of water and takes a sip. He looks over at his phone to see the time. He has been at the office since 7am and now it is a little past 9pm. Leo gathers his things and turns off the light to leave the building. After a little while longer, Leo finally leaves the office, walking towards his car from his office building, as he is the last one out. The office closes at 6pm now it's now around 9:45pm and it's been snowing on and off. There is about an inch of fresh snow on the ground. Leo has his hands full with briefcase, coat under his arm, and gloves in the other hand, glasses on top of his head. Leo places his gloves in his pocket as he searches for the keys to his car. The lot is completely empty outside of his vehicle. Everyone else went home hours ago and you can hear the wind in the night whistling. While searching for the keys another guy sneaked up behind him with an icicle in hand. Suddenly plunges the icicle into Leo's ear killing him instantly. Leo's lifeless body drops his briefcase and falls to the ground.

The killer with a portable hand dryer uses it on the snow eliminating the footprints. The killer never says a word. He had on a large green coat and black boots and gloves. The hood is pulled over his head where you can't see his face, only the coat. Small flurries start coming down making a fresh sheet of snow where Leo was killed. It looks like no one was ever around Leo. It just looks like a man lying on the ground. The cell phone in his pocket is ringing over and over. There are multiple missed calls and missed voicemail messages on his phone. Leo's wife stayed up waiting for him. She knows how hard he works, and she figures that maybe he fell asleep at his office. Leo has done it before. She waits as long as she can before she finally falls asleep.

The next morning a lady named Janet arrives at the office building. She is typically the first one to arrive at work every day. Janet is in her 50's always happy. Janet is the one who gets the music started in the office, turns everything on and prepares everything for all the workers. Janet parks her car and notices Leo car is still in the lot. Janet figures Leo must have stayed overnight working because that is the only way he would beat her to the office. Janet takes a lot of pride in being the first one to the office daily. Janet notices a body on the ground next to Leo's car. She can tell that it is Leo lying on the ground. Janet walks towards the body. She yells out his name LEO! LEO! LEO! Then starts to walk over towards him a little swiftly. As she gets closer, she realizes he is obviously dead and that he has been there overnight. Janet saw he was blue and had a little fresh snow around him. Janet realizing he is dead pulls her phone out and calls 911 as she looks around. Janet immediately thought that he overworked himself and probably had a heart attack or something. Leo worked so hard, and Janet would often tell him don't forget to eat or rest. She cries a little as she waits for the authorities and paramedic to arrive.

The first officer that arrives at the scene is Officer Jackson. Officer Jackson arrives at about the same time as the ambulance. Officer Jackson is a very serious person and has been a police officer for 15 years after retiring from the Army for 15years. He has always been a very good officer and has worked on many high profiled cases in the past. Officer Jackson just happened to be in the area and when he heard the call, he wanted to stop by to see if he could be of any assistance. Officer Jackson didn't really think based on the call over the radio that a potential heart attack case or a natural cause death would require much investigation, but figured since he was in the area he would try to help in any way that he could. Janet the office manager waives the paramedics and Officer Jackson over. The paramedics and Officer Jackson walks toward Janet and the body. Janet immediately starts to tell Officer Jackson and the paramedics that she walked over towards Leo to yell, to try to wake him but that she made sure not to touch anything because she knew that they would have to look at everything. Janet showed Officer Jackson her footprints and said that she kept everyone else away. The office manager Janet is single and watches a lot of police shows and wants to share all her knowledge from the shows with the officer.

She is very talkative, and Officer Jackson looks at Janet and tells her thank you thank you thank you. Calm down. Officer Jackson asks. What is your name? Janet says, oh, I am so sorry, Janet Kelly. I worked with the company for Officer Jackson cuts her off. Thank you, Ms. Kelly my Name is Officer Jackson, what is the guy's name over there. Janet replies. His name is Leo, and he is a very nice man he always Officer Jackson cuts her off again. What time did you arrive, Ms. Kelly? Please call me Janet I got here at 6:30 like I do every morning. I looked over and saw Leo on the ground; I yelled out his name and noticed that something was wrong. Leo was all blue and I saw the snow around him like he had been there for a long time. Janet starts to cry. Officer

Jackson puts his arm around Janet and tells one of the other officers that has now arrived to take her inside and that he can handle it from here.

A few other workers are starting to arrive now and are being instructed to go inside. Officer Jackson is looking at everything around the body to see if there is any foul play involved.

There is no evidence of anyone being there around Leo's body at all. Officer Jackson can see the small footprints of Janet and then of course the two paramedics. The icicle that was plunged in Leo's ear melted inside his head so there is no trace of a murder weapon and no fingerprints because the killer used the dryer to get rid of the footprints. Officer

Jackson continues to look and to him all he can see is a dead man lying in the snow. Looks like an unfortunate event. It doesn't look like there is any foul play involved. It looks like Leo just died naturally.

Other Detectives and CSI have arrived on the scene and are looking for some clues. Just as Officer Jackson thought the CSI see there are no clues at all. They see no footprints, no signs of a struggle, no weapons, nothing is stolen. Just a man dead by his car.

They figured that maybe Leo just had a heart attack, but he was healthy, and it seemed unlikely that he would have a heart attack. Maybe he had a lot of stress at work, and it caused a heart attack or something like that. It just looked like a normal death with no foul play. Nothing was out of place, so the CSI was wrapping things up.

The paramedic mentions to Officer Jackson that when they moved Leo's body, they noticed some blood out of Leo's ear that is frozen. They think maybe Leo fell and hit his head but there is no sign of him falling hitting his head or any abrasions on his head showing any sign of a fall or any struggle or anything. Just looks like a man passed away.

They figure maybe from all the work Leo must have burst a vessel in his head and just died. The coworkers are now all inside talking among each other. Janet speaks to them and says how nice Leo was and how unfortunate it was. Janet has an audience around her and you can hear the chatter as Janet is saying how she didn't touch anything around the body and how she helped the police out. Janet tells everyone that she thinks Leo just over worked himself and died from being over worked.

With no foul play being noticed there really is no case and everyone move forward feeling sad about the unfortunate death of a coworker. A specialist comes in just to look over everything to see if anything was missed or overlooked.

The specialist is a top Forensic Scientist/ CSI Agent Cabreena Adders that has literally the best eye for details and can see things most others can't. Agent Adders has worked on many cases and knows Officer Jackson. Agent Adders and Officer Jackson cracked a very high profile case together a few years ago and it was Agent Adders' amazing attention to detail that solved the case. Agent Adders is all over the scene. She is standing in silence just looking over the entire scene. Still not saying a word, she writes one word on a note pad. The word is "Why?"

Agent Adders has on a large CSI coat with the hood up and scarf on. Agent Adders has worked her way up to being the best. Almost 18years of service. She is not very big, but she has a commanding presence and is very well respected.

Agent Adders sees Officer Jackson and asks him "what's the verdict"? Officer Jackson says well, well, well. Look who is here. Long time no see. Good to see you. Agent Adders smiles at Officer Jackson and says same to you. Good to see you too. Last time I saw you we were working that case on the lady that was missing, and it was the neighbor. Talk about crazy! Officer Jackson say yeah that was crazy. Well, it looks like this one is not anywhere near as exciting as that one. It looks like the guy who died whose name is Leo was a good worker. He was found this morning by the office manager Janet. No foul play. By the looks of things, it looks like he just may have had a heart attack or something from over working and just dropped dead. Agent Adders say wow that is odd. Where is Janet? Let me ask her a few questions. Officer Jackson points in the direction and Janet and then tells the Agent. I don't know if it will lead to anything, but I know if there is anything at all, you will find it. Let me introduce you. Officer Jackson takes Agent Adders over to Janet.

Agent Adders goes to Janet and says hello Janet. My name is Agent Adders. Janet nods and smiles as she shakes her hand. Agent Adders says I am very sorry for the loss you have incurred, and I know this is not easy. I have a few questions that I am going to ask. Just a few routine things. Take your time and relax. Agent Adders asks Janet what was Leo working on in the office late. Is there anyone that has something against him? Any problems at the job or at home that you know of?

Janet replies Leo was loved by all, I am not sure exactly what he was working on, but it was pretty normal for him to work in the office for a long amount of time and late from time to time. It is just how Leo is. Once he is focused on any task, he just will not stop. Leo was very helpful and a good family man as far as I could tell. Pretty wife. He always talked about his family, and I know all the dirt but there was no dirt on Leo. He usually came in early and then basically lived in his office. Agent Adders said thank you to Janet then looked at Officer Jackson as they walked away as Officer Jackson mouthed the words "I told you" To Agent Adders.

Agent Adders speaks to detective Jackson outside and says yeah seems like a standup guy. I'm not sure if there is a perfect person, but if Janet knows anything, you know she would say it. You can tell that that woman will tell on anyone if she knows something about them. Both Agent Adders and Officer Jackson determine that they need to investigate what Leo was working on and maybe take a deeper look into how his family life was. Agent Adders says that she will go speak to the wife and asked detective Jackson to speak to the workers to find out more information about Leo. Agent Adders say I don't really think there is anything to find here but I just want to have every question answered just to be sure. Seems open and shut. Feel bad for the guy's family and friends.

Agent Adders went to speak to Leo's wife and tried to find out if there were any problems at home. At Leo's wife's house Agent Adders knocks on the door. The lady comes to the door. As she opens the door, you can see that she has been crying. Agent Adders goes to shake her hand and say Ma'am. Leo's wife cut her off and say call me Valarie, I know who you are, Agent Adders. Agent Adders say wow let me guess and at the same time, they both say "Janet". Valarie tells her. Yes, Janet called me already and told me who you were and everything. Valarie laughs a little through the tears and Agent Adders does a small laugh.

Agent Adders asked Valarie. Valarie, can you tell me about Leo?

Valarie said he was a devoted father and that they had a very healthy relationship. Valarie cried and just wanted to know what happened. Was it a heart attack or what was it? Why is a CSI Special Agent here? Was he killed or was it an accident? I don't know what to tell the kids. I just know that he was found dead by his car.

Agent Adders replies I am looking into everything to see what I can find out. By the looks of things, it seems like your husband was a good man and he worked very hard and unfortunately, he overworked himself and just died from either an aneurysm or heart attack. I am very sorry to have even come by to upset you. I am only trying to make sure I don't leave any stone unturned. I just wanted to make sure there was no foul play. If there was, I wanted to be able to bring whomever it was to justice and provide closure for you and your family. In this industry, I have seen a lot, and I only wanted to be sure that it truly was an unfortunate accident. Thank you so much for taking the time to even speak to me. I truly appreciate it. I will not bother you anymore. Valarie replies. I know that you are doing your job, and I know that it is not easy being the bearer of bad news. I do understand. It is just hard on me now. I still wish that Leo was here. Forgive me. Did you want anything to drink or anything? Where are my manners? Agent Adders replied. No need for you to apologize. You haven't done anything wrong. I am ok; I don't need anything to drink. I am going to leave now. If anything, else develops I will tell you.

I have one more question before I leave. How many times during the month, would your husband not come home and stay at work. Valarie cuts her off. Never did Leo cheat on me and there was never any other woman. I know what you are trying to ask. He was very dedicated. The one time I thought he was cheating, I went to his office just to see was he there and sure enough, he was there by himself working. Agent Adders interrupts and says again I apologize for being this way. I just must cover all the bases. I had to ask. Valarie now replies. Well, I must ask you to leave. Thank you and have a good day. Agent Adders nods her head and leaves.

Agent Adders calls Officer Jackson and say.
Well, I just left Leo's wife's house. Officer
Jackson asks so how did it go. Agent Adders
replies. Well, he wasn't having an affair,
seem like a good family man. I upset his
wife pretty much and got kicked out. Officer
Jackson replies back. Ouch that good huh?
Well, I am going to say what we are both
thinking. This is one where unfortunately a
good man just died. There is nothing here.
Agent Adders says you are probably right.
I am going to head back to his office just to
look around and see the parking lot once
again to see if I missed anything. Officer
Jackson says ok you do that. I think I am
going to call it a night. Agent Adders replies
ok talk to you later. Agent Adders hangs up
the phone and heads back to the scene. As

she is at the office in the parking lot just to look around again, she notices a man off into the background sort of watching but then suddenly walks towards the office. It is a little bit colder outside, and Agent Adders is bundled up as usual with her hood up and scarf half covering her face. The man has on a jacket with no hat on or gloves. His hair is a little disheveled.

She approaches the man and ask him if he worked at the place. The guy nodded then put his hands into his pockets to try and warm them up. Then Agent Adders asked him if he knew the deceased. The guy says yeah, I knew Leo, but I don't want to get involved. He starts to try to walk away swiftly.

Agent Adders starts to follow him a little, asks the guy for his name and then says get involved with what? What don't you want to get involved with? Is there something to be involved with? He walked away even faster without answering.

Agent Adders all bundled up from the cold decides to investigate the background of Leos work herself. She also wanted to investigate the guy she met at his job. She just didn't feel right about that guy. Agent Adders calls Officer Jackson and say. I met this weird guy today at Leo's job. The guy told me that he didn't want to get involved and walked well basically ran away. Officer Jackson says well it is kind of cold outside and people sometimes get weird about death. I think on this one you may be reaching a bit.

I will always trust your ideas and thoughts and if you want to investigate whom the guy is go for it. I just think there is nothing there. There were no footprints, murder weapon or motive for anything to happen to Leo. I can get you in contact with Janet if you want. She will positively know anyone that works there. Do it quietly though. You don't want people thinking you are holding a murder investigation. Agent adders say yeah yeah yeah. I got it. I will just tell her we are trying to close out the case. It will be fine. The following day Agent Adders sees Janet and say Hey Janet. I am just closing up everything and all my findings do you have a minute. Janet replies. Hey how's it going? Of course. Anything you need I am happy to help. Agent Adders found out that the guy that she met was named Milo after speaking to Janet.

She realizes that Leo was working on a project at his company and that things truly looked normal. Agent Adders was just confused and puzzled on his death. She just didn't know which direction to look. Agent Adders figures that the odd guy Milo is just an odd guy but nothing more.

A week goes by and still nothing. Finally, Agent Adders closes the book on Leo's death and has concluded he simply just died and that sometimes there is nothing sinister going on. Officer Jackson calls Agent Adders and asks. So how are you doing? It's ok. There are other bad people in the world that do bad things and you will be able to catch them. Agent Adders replies. It is just something off on this one and I just can't put my finger on it. I know that maybe I am just reading too much into it but for some reason I still have a feeling that there is something that I missed. No no no you didn't miss anything Officer Jackson replies. You are just used to being able to spot something and this happens to be a case that there is nothing to spot. You even said it yourself. The guy had a good family life and work life. Janet would have positively told us if the guy had anything else going on. Get some rest and the funeral is tomorrow. Please do not go to the funeral and upset that man's widow. Let them grieve in peace. Agent Adders say you are probably right. No way would I go to the funeral. Well it was good seeing you once again and working with you. I know we will work together again in the future. I have been in this for close to 18years. I don't know how many more years I can do this. Jackson replies well hey I have been doing this for so long I just stopped counting. I have been in the Army then all types of different areas in law enforcement. Now 15 more years of this. You are still young with a sharp mind. This business will eat away at you if you allow it to. You must look at each case and then file it and move to the next case. I know that a few years ago when we worked that other case and found out that the lady was killed by her neighbor it just ate away at you. You wouldn't stop until you cracked that case. The difference was that

that really was a crime and even though everyone thought that the ex-husband was the one who had to do it you stuck with only the facts of what the crime scene showed and never backed from the facts and evidence. That is what makes you great. No emotion was there on the feelings of the ex and how everyone was saying the ex-wasn't a good guy. You stuck with only evidence and that is what lead to you finding the zipper tab that popped off and had her DNA in it from her trying to fight back. No one would have ever noticed that. You found it. How did you even know to check the jacket? Agent Adders replies well I noticed in most of the neighbor's photos he always had that jacket. It was like a badge of honor for him since he got it when he tried out for a football team and made it. When I talked to him the first time, I saw all the pictures in his house and that jacket was always on in every important picture like it was an extension of him and his ego. Then after she was missing and no one could find her then when she turned up dead, he never seemed to wear the jacket again and I figured that was odd when someone who was identified by the jacket stopped wearing it, I wondered why. So, when I asked him about the jacket, he replied that the jacket wasn't that important and that he just figured it was time for a change. I asked him if I could see the jacket and he got it and put it on, I noticed that the zipper was missing. I asked him what happened, and he said the zipper had been off for several years and that is why he figured it was time for a change, but he kept the jacket because of football. He spoke so passionately to me about football and how he got the jacket and how only so many people ever got that jacket, and he went on and on. I figured that when he killed her, he probably wore the jacket and kept it even though he knew that was the only evidence. He couldn't part ways with it. If the jacket wasn't significant, he would have got rid of it. Then I thought if the jacket meant that much to him, he would have repaired the jacket. It hit me. He didn't repair the jacket because he couldn't find the zipper. He lied about not wearing it and the zipper being missing for years because just 2 days before she went missing the guy was out and took a picture with the jacket on. Then never again. When we found her body, one finger was missing some skin and the nail. I knew all I had to do was find that part of the zipper and he had the jacket in the house. I knew he would never part with that jacket. We knew that she was killed in her house then moved so when we checked the house and when they had all the evidence, I remember in the photos there was a zipper in the kitchen under the dishwasher but never thought anything of it. So, we got the zipper, got the DNA off it then got the warrant to get the jacket and that was it. See now that is the Adders that I know says Officer Jackson!!!! Following the evidence. That was huge. Well, I am glad that we took so many pictures of the house, other than that we wouldn't have ever had that chance. Well, I am about to go to sleep. Don't forget what I told you. Just do the case then file it and move on. The best thing was that through the entire story you never said the guy's name or the lady's name. You truly filed the case away. You need to do the same with this one. You are still talking about Leo as if he is still here and like there could be a suspect. File this away and don't let it eat away at you. Thank you for listening to me and for being there, says Agent Adders. I appreciate you a lot. Rest easy. Till next time. A few weeks go by and it's a light snow again and another guy name Vernon is walking from his car into his house. Vernon just finished a double shift at work and told his wife he would be home a little late. Vernon has the flowers that he got for his wife in his hand ready to surprise her. As Vernon walks up his walkway, a guy comes out the bushes from behind and with an icicle plunges it into his ear killing him. Once again, the killer uses the handheld heat Gun to melt away the footprints then of course the fresh falling snow covers everything up and there are no footprints anywhere to be found.

Vernon's wife Cheryl waiting for her husband to come home calls his phone with no answer then she calls again. Cheryl knows that Vernon said he was tired from the double shift but also, he said that he was on the way home. It is not like Vernon to ignore her calls or not even call her to say what happened. Cheryl calls one last time. Now Cheryl is very worried. She looks outside, sees his car down the driveway, opens the door, and notices Vernon's face down on the ground nonresponsive. She calls 911, the police, and the CSI agent Cabreena Adders and Officer Jackson, who is now Detective Jackson, comes again. Detective Jackson, and Agent Adders say first of all congrats on another promotion Lead Detective Jackson but, is this just some crazy coincidence or are you thinking what I'm thinking? Detective Jackson says thanks for the congrats and yeah. This is just crazy that another guy died exactly like the other guy a little while ago. Like some crazy Déjà vu. What is the likeliness of another guy being on the way home from work and then just dropping dead? No weapons, no motive, no foul play. Just a guy that has died. Agent

Adders say well to me it looks like we have a serial killer on our hands. This will not be it. We must catch this guy, whoever he is. Two people dying the same way is just too much of a coincidence. I knew from the very first one a little while ago something was off about it. I still can't put my finger on it, but I know that there is something going on. Something that we are missing.

Then Detective Jackson says who knows maybe it is just a freak accident that they both passed away? I mean there is literally nothing here to show us anything otherwise. No motive at all. No weapons or robbery. No sign of struggle. Just nothing at all. I am at a loss.

Agent Adders says look we don't want to get the town up in a frenzy and we positively don't want Vernon's wife Cheryl to panic but we need to find out what's going on before more bodies pile up. Detective Jackson goes over to talk to Cheryl. Hello, I am Detective Jackson. Just want you to try to describe to me if there was anything unusual about your husband's day or if he had any history of being sick or ill? Cheryl, crying and upset. I don't know! All I know is that my husband called me and told me that he was on the way home from working a double shift. Then after it took him too long to get home, I figured I would call him. Ok let me ask you this says Detective Jackson, does he always work a double shift? Did he over work himself and maybe that is how he died by accident? Cheryl replies. He doesn't usually work double shifts. He was just trying to work a little bit more so that we could save up some for a vacation to Hawaii. It is something we talked about for three years. Now he is dead. The paramedic said that it looks like he just had a heart attack or some type of brain hemorrhage. That just doesn't make any sense to me. My husband was very healthy. He goes to the gym 4 times a week. I don't understand that. I just want him back. Agent Adders walks over to the lady and shakes her head at Detective Jackson to let him know to back off and allow her to ask a few questions. Ma'am I am Agent Adders. First, I want to offer my condolences. I apologize for the questions. We are only trying to find out what happened to him and wanted to rule out anything sinister from happening. No way did we intentionally want to upset you. If you think of anything, please call me. Here is my number as she hands her a card. I'm just one phone call away. We will let you try to have peace as you go through this trying time.

Agent Adders then goes over to Detective Jackson to speak to him. Look

The first thing we need to do is see if Vernon and Leo knew each other or had any connection.

CSI officer Cabreena Adders is just looking at everything and is totally dumbfounded because there is just no evidence at all. Seems like there's not even a small clue.

The only footprints are those of the guy walking up to the house. There is no entry or exit wound from a gunshot. There is nothing taken from Vernon so there is no robbery. His car is still there, and he has the keys. No one went into the house to kill the wife. There is literally nothing. It truly looks like a case of someone just passing away. Agent Adders just can't accept it. She keeps looking around and trying to see if there is anything that she is missing. Detective Jackson is also confused by it. He says the likeliness of two men dying the same way just weeks apart is insane. Is it the weather because it is a little bit cold? Well, that doesn't make any sense because both guys have lived in the area for many years and the cold didn't do it. Detective

Jackson adds. Well both guys seem to have both been working extra hard and perhaps the body gave out and yes maybe a vessel burst in the head and that was it for them. It could really be something from just being overworked that really seems like it could be that. I am trying to see if there is something else but that is all that I see. I mean what is the motive? I don't see one at all.

Then Agent Adders notices in the background the same guy Milo from before that worked with Leo. She goes over to Milo, and he is visibly shaken. She says hey Milo tell me why you're here. Did you know this guy as well? Detective Jackson now walks over toward Milo and say. Well, she asked you a question. Detective Jackson is an intimidating force. Milo looks up still visibly shaken finally speaks with a trembled voice well umm ummm yeah I know him too, but I don't know about anything else. What happened to him? Detective Jackson asked, "Would you mind coming down to the station to answer some questions?" Is that a problem? Milo says well ok sure I guess that's ok. Detective Jackson says good let's go now. Milo ears are red from being outside in the cold once again with no hat or gloves on. Just a small jacket.

Back at the station Detective Jackson places Milo into the interrogation room and goes in first to ask some questions while agent Adders watches behind the glass. Right before any questions are asked the phone rings inside the interrogation room and it is Agent Adders on the phone telling Detective

Jackson to come out of the room. Detective Jackson goes to see Agent Adders, she tells Jackson to just wait for a little while and let Milo sit there for a while to make him sweat a little. Agent Adders says. This guy knows something, and we will find out what it is. Detective Jackson says oh I will get it out of him then goes back into the room. Moves the chair a little closer to Milo, sits down, rolls up his sleeves. Set a bottle of water in front of Milo. He asks Milo the question. We know that you know Leo from work. How do you know Vernon? Why were you out in front of Vernon's house this evening? It is not looking good for you Milo. I mean a guy at work dies and you're in the background watching. Now all of a sudden, another guy dies the same way and lo and behold, there is good ole Milo outside the guy's house. That is some kind of coincidence there isn't it, Milo? I really want to hear what you have to say because going to jail for two homicides is minimum 60 years for you to life. Milo, breathing heavy finally speaks. His hands shaking. He grabs the water bottle. Can't even focus to open it up. Then he blurts out. YES! YES! I knew both guys Leo and Vernon from college and that's it. Everyone kind of went their own way after college. Milo then opens the bottle of water and start to drink it like it is his last bottle of water he will ever have in his life. Not taking a breath at all. Just drinking the entire bottle.

The observant CSI Agent Adders noticed that as he was talking something changed and she could tell there was more and that he was lying. She calls Detective Jackson from behind the glass Detective Jackson picks up the phone. Agent Adders tells him to ask Milo why they went their separate ways after college and why they didn't stay in contact. Detective Jackson nods his head then hangs the phone up. He clears his throat and stares at Milo for about 40 seconds just to make it awkward. Then Detective Jackson speaks. So why didn't you all stay in contact after college? Why did you all go your separate ways? What happened? Whatever it was it was enough for you to come back and kill them?

Milo just kind of looks in a blank stare. Milo speaks again in a trembling voice. Look man I didn't kill anyone. You have got to believe me. Yes, I will admit once in a while we did talk but that is it. Detective Jackson asked well what did you all talk about? Did something happened in college? Is there something you're hiding? Milo didn't reply. Detective Jackson then says. I'll tell you what I think I think you're jealous of both guys because you all went to college together and you had the higher grades, but they are the ones who became more successful in life. They got the better jobs, the nice-looking wives and you were thinking wow that should be me! So, you decided to kill them both! You killed Leo so that you could advance at work and get his position. We looked it up. The project he worked on. A lot of it was your idea and you didn't get the credit that you thought that you deserved. Then on top of that Vernon's wife was your friend first and she ended up marrying Vernon instead of you. Wow two guys that are supposed to be your friend. One took your job and the other took your woman away. Yeah, that is why you killed them both!! Milo yells. That's not true!!! I earned that position, and Leo took it from me, but I wasn't angry at him and I didn't kill anyone. Vernon's wife was never my woman at all. That is not true. You are making up things about me. Detective Jackson then says wow you really got angry there. Do you want to hit me, Milo? If I wasn't wearing a badge, do you think you could take me? Do you have anger issues? Milo says no I don't but you're trying to make me seem guilty. Detective Jackson asks, "Do you feel guilty? Only people that can usually be made to feel guilty are the ones that are guilty. Innocent people don't say that they feel guilty because they don't know what guilty feels like because they are innocent. Are you telling me that you feel guilty or have remorse and maybe you want to tell me something? Milo says no there's nothing for me to feel guilty about.

Detective Jackson says you should go ahead and tell me what you know. Why were you at Vernon's house when he died?? Why were you walking around? Why is it that when someone dies you magically appear? Is it to see your handy work? Were you there to admire how good you are at killing? Were you there to mock us and rub it in our face that you are so smart, and we are so stupid that we will never catch you? Come on Milo, tell us the truth! Be a man for once. Say it! One guy took my job the other took my lady, so I took they life to get that job and take my lady back because I am a man!! Say it you ...Milo cuts him off any yells out I don't want to talk anymore without my lawyer!!! I'm done!!

Detective Jackson looks in the mirror knowing that Agent Adders is watching. He smiles and takes a deep breath. Looks back at Milo and rubs his hands through his hair and says ok Milo ok. You're free to go. Hey, Milo Just know we will be watching you. He says it will a very straight face while folding his arms. He then offers Milo another water, which Milo refuses and walks out after grabbing his jacket.

After Milo leaves Detective Jackson and Agent Adders talk. Detective Jackson asked. So, do you think I rattled his cage enough? Adders says. I don't think Milo's the one, but I think he probably knows who could be doing it and he will lead us to who's doing it. Yeah, I think you shook him up pretty good. I think he was about ready to crack. Detective Jackson says how can you be so sure that it's not him? I could see he was getting upset and wanted to do something. Then that guy asked for a lawyer. Who would even think to say that? Agent Adders said because whoever the killer is they are under control, very methodical and not sloppy enough to walk around the crime scenes to get spotted and look guilty. The Man we are looking for will be very smart and probably excels at whatever he does he will more than likely be a playboy or a bachelor. He will feel like he is too smart and slick to get caught.

Detective Jackson asks, back to the main question though.

Why? Why is the guy killing these guys? Why is there no murder weapon or anything at all? Maybe he is putting something in the food and then they drop dead later, and he watches them die? I just don't understand why. Then we are just really going off the deep end. Could it just really be that two guys died and ironically, they happen to know one another? I mean Milo has a good job and I just don't think he killed the guy for a job where he already makes a decent income and the other guy's wife being his girl was a stretch. I mean what would he even gain from it? This is the most insane thing I have ever seen before. A couple of guys dying, and no one saw anything. It's snowing and there are no footprints in the snow. No murder weapon/ guys just dying with no type of motive. Or has the guy figured out how to kill people with his mind! Agent Adders say Maybe it's something that is hidden from college and someone is trying to blackmail the other and it's some type of power move or some secret that can destroy a life. Maybe it is something like that.

Whatever it is. Milo is the key, and he will lead us to who's behind it.

Detective Jackson says I don't know how you figure things out but you've helped us solve multiple cases so I'll trust you and I will follow Milo to see where it leads us.

The following day Detective Jackson asked two officers just to keep an eye on Milo for the day and report what they see. The two officers are Officer Mayo and Officer Roth. They sit and wait. After a few hours they see Milo meet up with another guy and they seem to be having a heated conversation. Milo arms are up in the air. The officers can't make out what is being said but whatever it is they are positively not happy. Milo and the other guy walk away looking bothered both going their separate way. Officer Mayo looks at Officer Roth and says wow. Looks like Agent Adders and Detective Jackson were right. I wonder what those guys were talking about. We were told to watch Milo for the day. Tomorrow we will report what we found. Who knows, he could have just been having an argument with someone and it could be nothing. He looks like a pretty boring guy. Following him is not really leading too much. Oh, well we just follow orders. Easy money. They continue to follow Milo. Eventually nighttime comes and as they are staking out Milos place, they both fall asleep. Officer Roth wakes up and sees Officer Mayo sleep and hits him. Man, you were supposed to be up watching Milo while I took a nap. Officer Mayo says yeah yeah yeah. It's all good, nothing is going on anyway. I only nodded off for a few minutes. The lights in Milo's house now click on.

Then they see Milo coming back into the house, rushing through it. Officer Roth hits Officer Mayo once again and say. Man, you missed him leaving the house. We have no idea how long he was gone. What are we gonna tell Jackson now? Mayo replies. We are not gonna tell him anything. Not gonna have Jackson mad at me. No way. Well, let's just watch Milo to see what he does now. In the house Milo goes into another room. Pick up a phone, call someone then they see Milo once again looking bothered swinging his arms then he slams the phone down and the lights go off. Officer Mayo and Roth look at each other confused and Roth says this was a weird day following this guy around. Tomorrow we will report what we saw to Jackson and just leave out the you fell asleep part out. Deal? Mayo replies deal.

The following day another body is found. Detective Jackson and Agent Adders are on the scene again. Once again, the guy that is dead has no murder weapon by him, no sign of a struggle. Nothing is missing, no footprints or anything. Just a guy dead. Detective Jackson looks at Agent Adders and says this is just getting out of hand. They find out that the guy's name is Jeff. Officer Mayo and Roth show up on the scene to report to Detective Jackson about what they saw the previous day after following Milo. Officer Roth sees the dead man lying there then look at officer Mayo and they both sort of freeze when they see the body. Detective Jackson says well what happened when you all followed Milo? Spit it out! What is it? Officer Roth speaks up and says we saw the deceased guy with Milo yesterday. Jackson yells out WHAT!!! You all saw this man with Milo yesterday? How did this man end up dead today if you all watched Milo all day yesterday. Mayo instantly speaks up. He says sir it's my fault I fell asleep on the stakeout and when I woke up Milo was just entering the house. Yes, we saw that man with Milo earlier in the day having a heated discussion then Milo went home. We are not sure what time he left last night but he came back to the house around midnight and that is when he got on the phone for a little while before cutting the lights off and going to sleep. Officer Roth speaks up. Sir, it is not entirely his fault I also fell asleep.

Officer Jackson cuts them off. Whatever whatever!! Now there is another man dead and the guy that I told you all to watch that is probably the killer killed again and you all could have prevented it or saw how he did it. Agent Adders now speaks. She tells them, "Well the guy that is here name is Jeff and yes, he also knew Leo, Vernon and Milo. They all went to school together. Now he's dead. Jeff looks like he just dropped dead out of the blue. Jackson now furiously looks at both officers and says this is just unacceptable. We don't know if Milo is at risk or if he is the one doing it. If you all would have kept an eye on him maybe, we could have seen that maybe Milo didn't do it because you all were watching him. On the other hand, if it is him, you all could have prevented another man from dying. I need you all to go to Milos's house, job or wherever he is at, arrest him, and bring him in. Do you all think you can do that! This is a rhetorical question. Get out of my sight and go get him while I try and figure out what to tell this man's family after a third person has just dropped dead with no signs or reason. Jackson still angry turns and talks to Adders. Now we are starting to have the news reporters ask questions and want answers. People want to know if there is some pandemic going on that is causing healthy people to die. We don't need that type of press at all. People will get into a frenzy. We just got to go and arrest him. Adders talk to me. Tell me what you are thinking. The other officers Mayo and Roth leave to go get Milo. Agent adders say to Detective Jackson. What I am thinking is what is the motive for this if these guys are being killed? Also, I am thinking if it is Milo why would he kill again the next day after he knew you said you would be watching him. It just doesn't add up. I don't see Milo being that stupid to just up and kill again if he is the killer. We need to find out what happened at school and also how many others from this school could die? Is it going to be all men that went to the same school? How big can this thing scale? Is this guy that is killing just killing for sport? Could he not get into the school and want to kill everyone that went to the school. I mean that could be hundreds of people. We need to see how many other cases are maybe out there like this that we don't know about. Maybe other men have died the same way, and people just saw it as a tragic ending to someone dying too soon and just an accident. We could be the first ones to see a pattern and see that maybe something sinister is happening. Detective Jackson. Says you could be right! I never even thought of it that way. We have to talk to Milo. He got to know something. Let's get to the station and see if he can shed some light on this situation. I hope that it's not something that has been going on for years and years and people have just been seeing it as men having heart attacks from being over worked. We are going to have to go through a lot of paperwork. I will have the lady in the records department see if she can pull the deaths of people that just dropped dead and see if there is some pattern and if the guys all went to the same school. This could literally just be the tip of the iceberg. I am so glad that I didn't go to that school. I went to the army so I should be safe.

Now the officers Mayo and Roth are back at Milo's house. They arrest him, bring him to the station and in the car as they are taking Milo to the police station Mayo says it's amazing that we followed you a day ago then the following day that same person is dead and you're the last one to see him alive? Don't that seem a little strange to you Milo? What's going on? Milo is shocked to hear that he asks what happened to Jeff. Mayo says you tell us Milo. You tell us.

Don't worry; you will have plenty of time to tell your side of the story. Someone is waiting to talk to you. Milo shakes his head and says man there is no way that any of this will get put on me. I don't know why people are dying. I am just as confused. Whatever I will go through all this mess you all have me going through. I have nothing to hide. This is a waste of time. Whoever is doing something like you all keep telling me is not me. You just keep coming to me over and over. It is just exhausting. Now everyone in the car is silent and they continue to drive to the station as Milo looks out the window shaking his head.

Milo is back at the police station where once again Detective Jackson is waiting on him. They have Milo in the interrogation room once again. Milo just sits in the chair and still in disbelief just looked around shaking his head. This time Detective Jackson is oddly very very calm and stoic. He speaks. Milo Milo Milo. Wow, you have just become the most popular man of the hour. I'm sure that you've heard by now. Jeff is dead. That's right Leo, Vernon and now Jeff? Man, that is some body count that you are adding up. I had my officers follow you and you know what they found? I'll tell you. They saw you having a heated conversation with Jeff. Then they saw you storm off angry. Go home. Then they saw you rush out the house then come back into the house around midnight after killing Jeff then get on the phone and yell at someone else. Now I have two decorated officers prepared with a statement of what they saw. You may want to start talking buddy. I'd think hard about what words are about to come out of my mouth if I were you.

What are you hiding, why are you killing the guys you went to college with? What did they do to you? Was he trying to get money from you? We can pull the phone records to figure out what's the truth. How many more have you killed or will you kill. It's fine, no need to talk, I will just build the case the way that I want. Eyewitnesses saw you at multiple crime scenes, you talking to the victim and being the last one to see him alive. Then of course, your phone records, those will show us that you have been talking to them, probably making threats.

Ok ok ok ok I will talk Milo interrupts. Yes. Yes, yes yes we all knew one another. Are you happy now? Yes, we knew each other. It was the six of us that were always together growing up.

Detective Jackson looks over at the mirror and smile knowing that Agent Adders is watching from behind the mirror. Jackson looks back at Milo and grabs a seat then he tells Milo Please continue Milo.

Milo takes a deep breath and then he looks at the mirror knowing that others are watching. Milo then looks at his watch. Looks back into the air at the ceiling again. Then he puts his head on the table. Milo looks right into Agent Jackson eyes and very slowly speaks, "I did meet up with

Jeff, but it was to find out if he knew why the other guys were dying or getting killed and if anyone was saying anything. Jeff told me that he got a call that said, "It will all come to the light" "I know what you did. You need to pay."

Detective Jackson looks at the mirror confused then back over at Milo and asks. What will all come to the light? You also said six of us. Who are the other guys?

Milo puts his head down and starts to cry.

Just as he is ready to talk a lady walk in and says that's enough!!!!! I'm Milo's lawyer Regina Holmes. Regina is tall with an expensive business suit on looks like she just stepped out of a magazine for what a lawyer is supposed to look like. She hands

Detective Jackson her business card Holmes and associates. What are you charging my client with? Why is he here under arrest? Why is he here? Then she looks at Milo and tells him he does not have to answer any questions. Milo They are questioning you without any proof of anything and just trying to get some type of answer out of you to help them with a case that is bogus. She puts her arm out gesturing to Milo to come on then she looks at Detective Jackson. You should know better. Let's go Milo. Milo still crying, almost looking like he would rather stay there than go back on the street.

Detective Jackson said, "Well, he was the last one to see Jeff alive." Regina says, "What proof do you have of that? How do you know he was the last one to see him alive? What's his motive and how do you know anything. Please release my client now unless you have the proof to detain him".

The phone rings and it is Agent Adders. She tells Jackson to go ahead and let him leave. Something tells me he would rather be here with us than leaving. He looks scared. The next time we bring him in, he will tell us all that we need to know, and we will make sure no lawyers will be able to stop us. Jackson hangs up the phone looks, and Milo then looks at Regina. Looks back at Milo smiles and say, "You are free to go."

Milo leaves with the lawyer but you can see he is scared of something. Regina tells him as they are leaving Milo you don't have to let them question you. Milo replies. I know I know. I just want all of this to be over with. I don't know what's going on. The lawyer leaves, goes to her car and asks Milo. Hey Milo do you need anything? Milo look and say no I am ok. I will call you if I need anything. Regina rolls her eyes and speeds off.

As Milo is leaving the police station there are two guys outside waiting for Milo by a car and Milo sees them, he sort of froze. Milo looks around then nods to the guys for them to follow him. Milo walks around the corner into a coffee shop where the guys meet up with him. They sit and no one speaks for a moment. One guy is a muscular guy. Looks like he should be a model almost he has on a leather jacket designer shirt and boot cut jeans. The other guy looks like he belongs on Wall Street. Suit jacket pants with a topcoat. No tie with a white shirt. Hair slicked back, expensive watch and shoes. Finally, the first guy breaks the silence the more muscular one speaks. Man, who did you tell!!! Milo speaks. Ben, I didn't tell anyone anything. Milo looks at the other guy. Tyler, you got to believe me man. I didn't say anything at all. They are the other two guys from school Ben and Tyler. Tyler still has not said a word and he is just sitting there looking at Milo. Milo speaks again look guys I haven't said anything. Ben is always a little over the top and emotional says well someone seem to be killing us one by one with no trace or anything. If no one knows about it and it's just us three, which of us is doing it? Tell me right now, who it is because I'll take both of you out to save myself. I'm not going down without a fight. Ben speaks again. Look I don't care if someone is killing people that is on your conscious, but I am not gonna get killed or go to jail. If one of you all want to kill people that, is, your business. Just leave me alone. Don't come after me. I am not Vernon, Leo or Jeff. You not just gonna kill me and leave me on the streets. Just move on with life and let's end this right now. Now which one of you all is it? Milo I swear that if it is you, I will kill you myself right here.

Tyler is successful, methodical and always under control. He says look we need to remain calm because whomever it is they know everything about us, and we just need to find out what's going on. I don't think Milo is the killer because let's face it he's Milo. Also, Ben you are just an idiot and too over the top. No disrespect to you but it is who you are, and I know you couldn't do it because doing anything quietly is not in your nature. Then me I am me and why would I want to ruin my nice life and suits killing people that are below me. I know you all and neither of you will do anything. So, Ben calm down and stop making threats and Milo get a backbone. I think someone is obviously targeting us and must want something from us. I think we need to meet up somewhere else that is not by the police station. Let's meet up a little bit later this evening so that we can be in the same room to ensure we don't die and figure this out.

Milo nods his head as do Ben and they both say deal. Then Milo said, "Wow did you really have to tell me to get a backbone. Ben laughs, Milo tells Ben don't laugh too hard he called you stupid and over the top. Ben stops laughing, looks at Milo and says at least I have a backbone. Milo shakes his head and looks at Tyler and says yeah, you're right let's get outta here.

The CSI Agent Adders is watching the three guys along with Detective Jackson. Adders says there is something going on. I guess those are the other two guys that Milo said were a part of the six of them that hung out. Those are the missing pieces. We need to get all of them and pull them into separate rooms where they all see one another go in. One of them will break. I am sure of it.

I am going to wait behind the mirror again to watch all three of them. I want you Mayo and Roth to have each one in a separate room to question. This will work. Jackson nods his head in agreement and says ok let's close this case. One of those idiots are the killer. This will end today.

The three guys Milo, Ben and Tyler leave the coffee shop. The officers Mayo and Roth along with Detective Jackson are waiting and apprehend all of them and pull them back into the police station where they all see each other going into different rooms. Ben, Tyler and Milo, all look at each other right before they go into the separate rooms. The guys are all sitting in individual rooms looking around. Milo actually looks relieved. Ben looks very tense, and Tyler is as cool as a cucumber. Just sitting there looking in the mirror waving and smiling. Then Tyler blows a kiss at the mirror. Ben is in his room now he starts yelling out. Ok let's get this show on the road I got a couple shows I want to see on TV. Let's go. I ain't got time to be sitting here playing games all day. Agent Adders tells detective Jackson to start with Milo and tell him we know it's him. I'm telling you Jackson he is ready to break start with him. They have also found out that the other guy's names are Ben and Tyler. Jackson says yep, I agree let me go crack this egg. Jackson walks in the room and tells Milo we already know it's you. Ben and Tyler said that you're the one who's doing it and trying to get money out of the others to remain quiet. Do you want to go ahead and cut a deal now so that you don't get the death penalty? Over in the other room officer Mayo tells Tyler guess what buddy? Ben and Milo are cutting a deal right now as I speak to you. They told the other officer that it is you doing the killing and that you've asked them for money to remain quiet. Tyler is not flinching and laughs. Nice try however no way is that the truth. In the other room Officer Roth tells Ben we know it's not you. Which one of them is it? Who in your mind do you think it is? We already have confirmed that there is no way that it can be you.

Then CSI Agent Adders calls Officer Roth on the phone. Officer Roth picks up the phone and Adders tells Roth to tell Ben we know what happened in college just tell us who's the one doing it. Tell him we know that he didn't mean for anything to happen. Roth replies. Got it.

Officer Roth hangs up the phone, turns to Ben and speaks. Ben, we know what happened in college I just got the call man. You have got to just tell us your side so that it doesn't get any worse than what it already is. This all need to stop now man. Just let it go.

Ben always quick to react with his emotion breaks down and says we didn't try to hurt her man. We were just having fun. (Officer Roth is shocked and has no idea what he's talking about, but he goes with it).

Yes, we know you all didn't mean to do it. It's not your fault man. Just tell me what happened.

Ben says man we were all at the party in college. The girl was hanging out with us she seemed into it. She told us that she felt a little dizzy and that maybe she should leave. Then Leo was like no no no you don't have to leave we are just getting started. He yells out "Who got condoms? Let's have real fun. Then Vernon, Milo, Jeff and Tyler start holding her down. The girl was crying and kept saying stop stop stop. She said I want to go I just want to go. She said please don't do this to me please. I told them to stop but they just took turns jumping on top of her. Then Leo told me I had to get in there too or they would tell on me. They said they wouldn't let me leave the room if I didn't participate. They said you know that you want to man. It's all just fun. Nothing is gonna happen. She wants it. I told the girl I was sorry. I started but then I stopped. All the guys laughed at me and said that I couldn't handle a woman. That is when Leo said that's ok just means more for me. Then he started choking the girl and told her to shut up. He slapped her and started asking if she liked it. Once he got up, she wasn't moving or breathing. Then Vernon said man I can't find a pulse. That is when everyone panicked. I told them we need to call someone. They said whom can we call and what would we say? They told me to just shut up and see if we can get her breathing again. Then Vernon said he thought he found a small pulse and panicked. We made a pact and said we would never speak of it. Then Milo was the one who forced everyone to do everything for him and everyone did whatever he wanted out of fear that he would tell. Milo and Jeff decided to bury her in the snow and make her a live snowman and thought it would be funny. They said well she was passed out and that the next day when she woke up, she wouldn't know what happened and probably won't say anything because she was a freshman anyway. I mean who would believe her? Then Jeff said yeah, she wasn't even drinking alcohol she said all she wanted was water, but he put a little something extra in her water to make her loosen up and have fun. He said it's what happens to freshman all the time and that she would be stronger from it. No harm at all. Besides, we wore protection, and she had a good time. She just don't know it as he laughed. After we buried her, then none of us ever talked about it again and we didn't see the girl again. I don't even know if she died or not. I just knew that it would be reported to the police or something, but nothing happened and we just kind of moved on with life. Then Milo kept bringing it up as time went on.

Milo for the rest of our lives he's always had us give him money, get him set with jobs or anything else. The person that I think is killing everyone honestly is Tyler, he is the one killing us one by one so that he don't lose his job and family and all the fancy stuff that he has. Plus, the pressure of always getting calls from Milo. I think he snapped and is killing everyone. He's tired of Milo, I know it.

The officer asks Ben. Why are you not the killer why can't it be you? It's not me because I never wanted anything to happen in the first place and I just couldn't wait to get this off my chest. I want to stay safe because I think he will kill again. He's always been the one that plans everything and says how smart he is. Good ole Mr. Perfect Tyler.

Then Officer Roth steps outside to talk to Agent Adders and since the rape was never reported or nothing was ever documented or spoke on, they can't even determine if the story that was told was true. Agent Adders say that is some story but there were never any reports or anything of any rape plus the guys that got killed had good family lives. Who knows if he is just giving us a story to save himself? I am going to pull out Jackson and Mayo and see if they can question Milo and Tyler to see if they say yes to the same story. Agent Adders calls Jackson and Mayo in and has Roth tell them about the story that Ben told him so that they could go tell it to Tyler and Milo to see if they confess as well. Officer Roth tells them. Man, Ben told me that they raped some girl in college. He didn't know the girls name and said that they beat and raped her, and that Ben thought she was dead but then they found a small pulse and ended up burying her in the snow, ben said that after burying her in the snow then they never heard any police reports or anything else from the girl. Never even saw the girl again. Ben said that the girl had just vanished. He said that he didn't know if she died in the snow but there were never any body found or anything and the guys all just kind of went on with life. Crazy story, right? Aw wait the other part too it is that he said that Milo was extorting money and stuff out of everyone, or he would tell on them and destroy their lives. Ben then said that he think Tyler got tired of the calls from Milo and threats from people and decided to kill everyone one by one so that there would be no witnesses. So that is the wild story from Ben. What do you guys think? Detective Jackson says good job Roth. I am going to go with the story and Mayo, you and I need to go in and see what Tyler and Milo got to say about it and the truth will come out. Adders what do you think? Agent adders say what I think is that one of these guys are the killer and we need to find out how they are doing it if we want anything to stick because telling a story about a non-reported rape with no witness or evidence is never going to stick. We need to break them and need someone to say how they are killing the guys without any murder weapons or any sign of struggle or foul play. We have to get something concrete. I need you guys to go in and get how they are doing the killings. I feel bad hearing about a rape but if it wasn't reported and no witness came forward how can any of what this guy say be proved. He actually seem like he will say or do anything to save himself. I think Milo could be the killer, but Tyler is so calm and methodical it could actually be him because his personality seem like he would be best suited to kill people in a slick way where no one could prove it. Ben seems like if he was killing people it would be with brute force. Milo just seems a little timid. Adders tell them fellas go in and press them and get the evidence on how they are doing it. That is how we will nail them. All the officers look and nod then go back into the rooms.

Now Mayo and Jackson go to the separate rooms to speak to Tyler and Milo about the rape. Mayo tells Tyler we know about the rape. The secret is out Tyler. You may as well tell me your side of the story. Tyler instantly points the finger at Ben he has now lost that cool calm demeanor that he had. He is now in pure survival mode. He says no no no officer. It was Ben all the way. He's the strongest of all of us. He raped the girl then had us live in fear that he would say that one of us did it and not him. I think Milo got mad at being pushed around by Ben and I think he said something to Ben. I think Ben then got mad at Milo and started to kill everyone one by one to keep us in line. It has to be Ben. Over in the other room Detective Jackson is talking to Milo he says, ok Milo they are saying that you raped a girl and then tried to get hush money. They are saying that it is you. Milo looks totally stunned because the secret is out. Instantly Milo Points the finger at Tyler and say Tyler is always the smooth leader of the group he raped the girl while Ben held her down then they made me watch. I think that Ben got tired of being the muscle for Tyler and he is the one killing everyone because Tyler calls him stupid all the time and he want to show he is not stupid. The guys are all pointing fingers at each other. While they are their Agent Adders had warrants for each guy's house and have sent police officers to each guy's home to see what can be found. The other officers are checking out the houses of each guy. They noticed in Milo's house. Photos of each guy, what time they work, where they live, then they see a few different variations of demands and dollar amounts with a promise to make them hurt or pay in other ways including messing their lives up. The other officers are back and have the evidence of Milo's home showing he's the one that has the photos, and dollar amounts and the different threats he had saying what he can do to ruin people's lives. Looks like Milo was the one. Now Detective Jackson officer Mayo and Roth get together leaving the guys in the rooms to just sit and wait while they compare notes. Jackson says wow we had the guy all this time. It was Milo. I knew that it had to be him. Now we just must have him actually tell us how he is killing people without a trace. I have never seen anything like this in my life. Detective Jackson has the yearbook and all the information on where the guys went to college and any information on them that he requested the day before. He looks at the other officers and say fellas it looks like this case will be closing soon. I got all this information. If you all want to go in and talk to the guys so that we can start to wrap this up. It shouldn't take that long to piece it all together. I will get with Adders once we get the confession, and we will be ready to close it down. However, boys. There will be a lot of paperwork to put this report together so be prepared for a long week. Detective Jackson fist bumps both officers and the other two walk into the rooms to talk to Ben and Tyler.

They are looking at the notes and it seems like Milo has to be the killer. They are going into Ben and Tyler's interrogation room to tell them the good news. However once they go back to the rooms Ben and Tyler are already dead!!! Officers Roth and Mayo run out the rooms yelling out to Jackson saying Jackson Ben and Tyler are both dead!!! Jackson looks towards Milo's room and run in with his gun drawn and see the room is empty! Milo is gone!!! Milo who they assumed was the bad guy seems to have killed Ben and Tyler and he has obviously escaped. Jackson yells out Lock it down!!!! Mayo and Roth scramble out and they are yelling into the walkie-talkies. Prisoner has escaped. He is considered armed and very dangerous. Milo Gibson has escaped. Be advised he has killed 5people that we know of. Everyone is running and out now on a manhunt to catch him. They know who the killer is and are hunting him down. While they are looking for him, Detective Jackson looks at the clips to see if there is anything on the camera. All he can see is Milo leaving the station very grainy footage of the back door only shows Milo leaving. The cameras in the rooms weren't on and there is no murder weapon just as the others that died. Just two guys laying there dead. Blood running out of the ear. Nothing else. Jackson is reading through the files seeing if he can see anything in the notes that he has overlooked.

Outside the police station now, it is shown that Milo is in an old ice-making warehouse and he wakes up a little dazed. He is sitting in a chair. We now see the same guy from the beginning that killed the others walking towards Milo. Milo is sitting in the chair begging for his life. The killer walks up slowly. Then Milo looks and sees the face and he's like you? Why are you dressed this way? Why you? It's the CSI officer Cabreena Adders she pulls off the larger man shoes she was wearing over her shoes. She pulled off the large man's coat that she wore in the beginning to kill Leo with and Vernon. Now she is walking towards Milo. Adders says you all raped me, beat me, drugged me buried me, and left me for dead and went on to live your lives like you never did anything at all. I had to leave that school. I never told anyone about it because I knew they wouldn't believe a freshman. I was only 17years old. My 18th birthday hadn't even come yet. Because of you all, I can never have kids or any type of a family. My entire insides are messed up. It took me 6 months to learn how to walk again. I suffered hypothermia and had to have a part of my toe amputated. I have no feeling in my fingertips. I had to go to counseling for 2 years. It's ok though. I never reported anything at all. I ended up leaving the school and prepared for this moment for 17years. I found a way to eliminate all of you. I studied and studied and followed all of you guys for all these years. I had so many chances to kill all of you, but I wanted it to be perfect. It's almost done now. As Milo is in the chair trying to apologize. She goes over plunges the icicle into his ear killing him. Then she takes him to the ice machine and buries him under the ice machine the way she was buried years ago.

Back at the station the Detective Jackson is listening to the tape again and he listens to the last part again

Ben said, "We never saw the girl again, we looked for articles on it in the paper somewhere and it never came up. We went back to where we made her a snowman and she wasn't there. We have no idea whatever happened to that girl at all. It's like she vanished into thin air".

The officer sits and thinks. As he replays everything in his mind, he realizes that CSI Agent Adders was never in the room with the guys. She always sent someone in to talk to the guys for her as she watched.

He thought about the first time she met Milo she had her head covered and the hood over her face. Milo never saw Agent Adders. As Detective Jackson looks back at what school the guys went to then he looks over the file on Agent Adders and looks up what college she went to. Jackson discovers that for her freshman year one semester she went to the same school as the guys before transferring. Her major changed and she started to study forensics. Detective Jackson thinks about when they were interrogating the guys. It was her idea to get them to talk about college and confess. He sees that she just wanted them to confess what they did to the girl and perhaps the girl is her. That was what it was all about. It had nothing to do with the murders or finding out who did them. It was all set up to get them to confess. That was her plan. Now detective Jackson see it. It is only a theory that he has but, Detective Jackson goes to CSI agent Adders house and uses the spare key she gave him for emergencies. Opens the door. He sees the large coat hanging and the oversized boots that are wet. Detective Jackson see a pouch and opens it, inside he see two sharp icicles. He walks over into the other room where Adders just came from the shower; hair still wet and robe on. She looks at Detective Jackson. Not really surprised but just a simple smirk and ask. So did you find Milo? Detective Jackson ignores the question throws her file on the table and he says so they beat raped and buried you that was the motif? Adders look at Jackson then starts to speak. I didn't get raped or buried. I got drugged when I was 17. I then was brutally raped by six men over and over. They took turns choking me and beating me until I passed out. And every time I came too, they beat and raped me again. I was not at a party. One of the guys asked me if I wanted a tour of the school because it was a big school. I said wow thanks that's nice. He then offered me a bottle of water. Once I drank the water and woke up they were all taking turns with me. That wasn't the first time they did it. They did it to multiple girls. Then they actually killed one of the girls and got away with it. The other girls they paid off or humiliated them so badly that they never came forward. With me, they thought they killed me and tried to bury me. I thought I was dead too. When I came too I was frozen under ice and I couldn't feel my toes and didn't realize one of my toes were so frozen that I broke them. I just kept yanking my body until I freed myself. Then I ran until I got to a street and passed out. Someone I don't know who it was picked me up and took me to the hospital as a jane doe. After I gained consciousness. They asked me what happened and that is when I found out that my insides were so messed up that I could no longer have children. I also found out that they had to amputate a part of my toe and replaced it with a piece of flesh so that I could still stand straight. I have no feeling in my fingers. I had to go to therapy for years. It changed my entire course of life.

Then I look up and see those guys living great lives. I found out that they did it to countless girls and one of the girls died. They needed to be gone. Detective Jackson has tears in his eyes after she speaks. Then he wipes them away and speaks.

You wanted it all to get out. You wanted them to confess. You never reported the rape so there could be no record of it. Amazing that your first year of college was at the same place as those guys. What better way to get away with murder and forensic evidence than be a forensic scientist and become a CSI agent. Talk about a perfect profession. I get it and it was very bad what happened to you. I still don't know if I can allow someone to just get away with murder. I still have a job to do. It looks like Milo did it. We got all the evidence from his house. Showing how he was getting the guys to give him jobs and pay him off to keep him quiet. He was the only one really with nothing to lose so he exploited that with the other guys. I think that he got scared when the guys started dying and he was trying to figure out who was doing it, that is why he was at the crime scenes. You decided to make the focus go to him. Very smart. Now he's vanished. I guess that the case is closed. He escaped and he is on the run.

Or I can present what I think even though there were never any documents of rape or anything and all the so called guys involved are dead and one is on the run/ missing. I assume we won't find that guy? Yeah there is no way that I can actually question anyone to validate the rape case because all the so-called parties are dead or missing. Then the deaths of all the guys never had a murder weapon retrieved. No footprints I am still trying to figure that one out. How in the world did you even do it? Or I can say that you must have done it.

She turns to him smiles and say that's good. She turns on her hand held dryer to dry her hair. She turns the dryer off and then she takes the case with the icicles and put them into the sink and let the water run on them. She looks at her hand held dryer. Turns it back on. Then Agent Adders smile again and talks over the dryer and say that is some theory. After the icicles melt she turns off the hand dryer and look at the detective and say it's amazing how the hand dryer gets rid of things that are wet like maybe footprints in snow or dry hair. I don't know what could have killed the guys. Maybe an icicle getting plunged into someone's ear. Who knows? You have put a very interesting case together with a lot of probabilities. Too bad the killer is still on the run. Detective Jackson say yeah who knows. Not sure what I should do. Agent Adders then replies. Well detective looks like you have a choice to make. I just have one thing to say.

Prove it?

THE END.

Milton Keynes UK
Ingram Content Group UK Ltd.
UKHW041945091024
449514UK00005B/26